For Joseph

JOSEPH
and the
ROPE BRIDGE

Written by Patrick FitzSymons
Art by Donna FitzSymons

PUBLISHED BY OMSQUAD BOOKS

Published 2011 by Omsquad Books
21 Moycraig Road, Dunseverick, BT57 8TB
© Patrick FitzSymons and Donna FitzSymons

Design by Donna FitzSymons
Printed and bound by SS Media Ltd
Cardinal Point, Park Road,
Rickmansworth, Hertfordshire, WD3 1RE
ISBN 978-0-9565517-1-9

'Imagine a walk in the air, carried along on a fresh wind.

The birds soaring above - and below you.

And down there, between your feet, the sea, dark blue and green,

rising and falling.'

Joseph stole a glance at his big cousin, as they walked along the cliff path.

She was just teasing him again, wasn't she?

But when he saw it, he simply stared.

It was indeed the most amazing bridge he had ever seen.

It seemed to hang in space, stretching out

over the churning sea, toward the dark cliff opposite.

It looked like... an adventure!

'This is our bridge,' said Morgaine. 'Do you want to go across?'

Joseph was itching to, but held back. 'Is it safe?'

'Of course!' Morgaine laughed.

'Someone went across on a bicycle once.'
Joseph looked at her like she wasn't all there.

'They did,' Morgaine grinned. 'And another man walked across ... on his hands!'

'Folk round here have been using the bridge for hundreds of years.'

Joseph looked uncertain. 'Is it really old then?'

'No, silly. They change them. The 'oul ones were much more wobbly.

But this one's great.' Morgaine put on her serious face

and cocked her head to one side. 'So, what do you think?'

The little boy was already squeezing past her.

'Me first!'

The wind fanned their faces as gulls rode the air around them,
flying to and from their nests on the jagged rock.
Morgaine kept an eye on her little cousin, as he put one foot in front of the other,
clutching the thick ropes and staring down at the waves
rushing in under their feet.

'I wouldn't want to be here if the volcano exploded again.'
Joseph looked back over his shoulder. 'What volcano?'
'The one down there,' Morgaine pointed to the sea below.
'All this burny stuff comes shooting out of the ground
and boils you!' she beamed.

Joseph walked a bit more quickly.

'And when it cools, that's where all the browny-coloured rock comes from. Granddad told me the volcano plonked the island right in the middle of the salmons' road...

...and that's why the fishing was so good here.
He says he and his da could hardly pull them out fast enough!'

Stepping off the bridge and along the island path,
the children looked down at the old fisherman's cottage.
If they'd been around back then, they'd have been working here too,
maybe sitting on the slope mending nets,
or helping with the crane that lifted boats
in and out of the water.

They thought about their Granddad as a small boy,
loading fish into the creel his father would carry on his back.
Together, they might take the catch home
or perhaps up to the ice house on the road above the village.

Joseph pointed to
the other side.
'Look at all the people coming.'
'Oh aye.' Morgaine put her
hands on her hips.
'They've been coming
for donkeys' years
to see Carrick-a-rede.

You can see them
in all the old photographs.
As long as folk have had cameras.'
'Carrick-a-rede? Is that what you call it?'
'Aye!' said Morgaine. 'Most folk do.
But me and Grandda call it
McCurdy's Bridge.'

'Have our family always been here?'Joseph asked.

'Forever.' said Morgaine. 'Even back when people made all their stuff out of stone, some of them were McCurdys.'

She pointed toward the white cliffs of Larrybane.

'Ma says, when she was a we'an, she found a stone axe over there, with no handle on it.'

'What's a 'we'an?'

'You are.' said Morgaine. 'A kid.' She shook her head.

'You city ones. You know nothing.'

'Are you a we'an? Joseph wondered.

'Course not.' Morgaine tutted. 'I'm nine!'

'You know what the McCurdys have to do, though?'

Joseph said nothing as she leaned a little closer.

'There's a monster lives in a cave near here,

with curly horns and teeth like pointy rocks and eyes like boulders.'

'I don't believe you.'

'It's true. It comes out every odd while to scare the folk of Ballintoy...

and it loves the taste of we'ans!'

The little boy looked at his cousin side on.

'Only McCurdy men can fight it,
when it shows its ugly bake.'
She paused, her eyes narrowed.
'So you would have to -'
The words froze
and she spun around.
'What was that?'
'I didn't hear anything.'
Morgaine crept down the path.
'Listen. There it is again.'
Slowly, she turned back.
'I think it's... the monster. Aargh!'

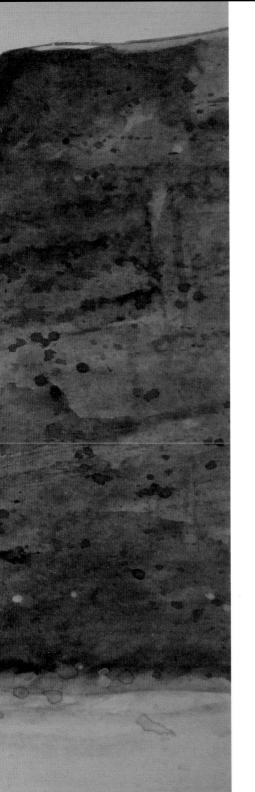

And together they ran, laughing, back to the bridge... and home.